Amanda Hubbert
Illustrations by Marina Greeves

To logan

Love Amanda

Roho and Rafiki

Bumblebee Books
London

A CIP catalogue record for this title is
available from the British Library.

ISBN: 978-1-83934-170-0

Bumblebee Books is an imprint of
Olympia Publishers.

First Published in 2021

Bumblebee Books
Tallis House
2 Tallis Street
London
EC4Y 0AB

Printed in Great Britain

www.olympiapublishers.com

Dedication

To my daughter and the people that truly believed in me.
I thank you.

Roho was only a few hours old.

She was born in the zoo at teatime on a Friday in late May. She already weighed a hundred and fifty pounds and when she stood up for the first time she was an amazing six feet tall. Roho was a baby giraffe.

Her ears were alert, taking in her new surroundings. She lived with six other adult giraffes in a very large enclosure. There was plenty of space for Roho to play.

One Saturday afternoon, Roho was out exploring her surroundings and looking at the other types of animals that were the other side of the fence. They ohh-ed and ahh-ed as they walked past.

Roho was alone. As she looked around, there were lots of strange noises around her and the loudest came from the trees above.

There on the lowest branch was a feathered animal with a white head, sharp grey beak, small round black eyes, and the most amazing royal blue feathers.

His tail was aqua blue, thin feathers that split in two to form two small points like a humming bird's beak.

The noise she heard seemed to come from the feathered animal. Roho wanted to find out if the animal was okay.

Roho nudged the animal with her nose.

"Hey!" he shouted.

"Sorry," said Roho. "I was just making sure you were okay."

"I'm learning to sing like my brothers and sisters. They are all really good at singing. I can't get the notes right when I sing as a family," the feathered animal sighed.

"My mum sent me down here to practice on my own." He dropped his head low but continued to talk. "They say I sound like a child screaming around the zoo!"

"Come on, it's not that bad. Let's go for a walk and you can tell me what 'children' are," Roho said as she turned.

"My name is Rafiki. I'm a blue-bellied roller bird, and I come from Africa," he said. He cheered up and flew after Roho. He caught up and landed on her head as they walked.

The two new friends chatted all the way around the enclosure. Roho learnt a lot about all the different things around her.

She found out that the other animals the other side of the fence were called humans and the small ones were the children.

All of a sudden Roho heard a dull thumping noise and the ground seemed to shake; then came the screaming and lots of shouting.

"What is that?" Roho asked.

"That will be the children's birthday party. They will look at you, then run off to the next enclosure. They never stay long in one place, and the adults then rush after them all over the place."

"Well you definitely don't sound like them when you sing, Rafiki. Your family are wrong," Roho said as they headed back to Rafiki's tree.

Roho had an amazing first day with her new friend. She learnt so much. She had not realised how many different animals lived in the zoo.

Roho was being called into the shed by her mother. Rafiki flew up into his tree shouting, "See you in the morning."

"Where have you been all day?" Rafiki's mum asked as Rafiki landed in the tree.

"Oh, just meeting a new friend. You know I like to meet the new animals in the zoo," he replied.

Rafiki was told to settled down for a sleep, but he was way too restless and couldn't wait to see his new friend.

He waited until his family was asleep and flew down to the giraffe enclosure.

Roho was wide awake too. She was excited to see Rafiki but had to keep the noise down as the others were snoozing.

"Oh, good. You're awake," whispered Rafiki so he did not wake the others.

"I'm far too excited to sleep. I have seen and heard so much," Roho said in a soft voice.

Rafiki told Roho about how the different animals that live in the zoo come from all over the world, and the humans many years ago caught the animals for the other people to see.

This surprised Roho and she wanted to know more. She wanted to meet the other animals and find out if they too were born in the zoo or they were trapped to live here.

Her mind was full of questions. It felt like it was going to burst. She had no idea how she was going to find out about these animals and answer the questions swamping her mind.

Rafiki got a sparkle in his eyes as he started to fly back to his tree. He turned and said, "Well, maybe you can with a little bit of magic. We could see the world together."

Roho stared at him. "What do you mean?"

"I will tell you in the morning, but for now you need some sleep." And with that, Rafiki was gone.

Roho was far too excited to sleep that night. Before she knew it, the keepers were at the door and opening up the paddock. Fresh food had been put out to each hanging basket.

As soon as Roho had eaten something, she was off on the hunt for Rafiki.

She had so many animals she wanted to meet but where to start and how?

She greeted Rafiki with a mammoth amount of words that really made no sense to a small blue bird. They all seemed to merge into one long sentence. She was so loud when she talked to Rafiki. He thought she sounded like one of the over-excited children that run past.

There was so much to learn but that was going to have to wait. In the distance, she could hear the stamping of feet on the ground. The visitors were coming to see her and the family of giraffes and all the others animals in the zoo.

The day went so slowly for Roho. She couldn't believe the amount of people who stopped to look at her. She had no time to talk to Rafiki. She paced up and down, wishing the day would be quiet and soon come to an end so she could talk to her friend.

It was lunchtime when everyone seemed to go off for picnics, and the enclosure was calmer so that Roho got to speak to her friend Rafiki.

Rafiki flew down from the other side of the paddock and landed on her head.

"Hello," cheeped Rafiki in a sing-song mood.

"Hi ya," said Roho. "I'm glad you landed—" That's all she got to say as more people were hurrying around the enclosure, and cameras were flashing all around. The keeper's voice came on loud around the enclosure. It was time for the keeper's talk.

Rafiki flew off into the tree while Roho stood by her mother.

Finally the day came to an end and all the humans disappeared.

The zoo became quiet of pounding feet and screaming little ones, all that could be heard was the birds tweeting in the distance, a lion roared making Roho jump and turn around fast.

It was so loud it was like it was behind her.

Rafiki landed on Roho's head which made her jump and move fast across the paddock.

Rafiki flew up in the air and was laughing hysterically as Roho finally came to a stop near a tree.

"What are you laughing at?" Roho snapped in a grumpy voice.

Rafiki flew down and landed on the lowest branch of the tree and he was still laughing.

Roho tried to knock him off using her long neck, but instead she lost her balance slightly, which set them both off laughing.

They both stopped when another roar ripped through the zoo like lightening through the sky.

"Why is that lion so loud?" Roho questioned.

"He is hungry," replied Rafiki. "Would you like to visit him?" Rafiki continued.

"Emm, no thank you! He may try to eat me." Roho paused. "What do you mean, go visit him? Is this what you were talking about last night?"

Rafiki smiled as he spoke, explaining that he could take Roho to visit the lion's den and see what all the noise was about.

Roho looked scared. Rafiki continued to talk. "It's okay, we can stay outside, and no one will see us."

Roho smiled weakly and Rafiki started to chant these words: "I want to see the lions in the zoo, up close and personal so we can learn all about you." And whoosh they were both gone, inside the lion's enclosure.

Roho froze and turned her head slowly to see where they were.

"We are inside!" she shouted. "But he can't see us, can he?" Roho was panicked.

"Well," Rafiki began, "yes, he can see us. It's just people who can't." Rafiki then flew into the air to get a better view.

Roho spun her head around to face Rafiki, but he was gone.

That's when Roho spotted the lion. He was crouched down in the long grass, camouflaged, very hard to see, but Roho saw him looking at her with a greedy smile.

"Rafiki," Roho choked out a squeak, she repeated it again. "Rafiki." On the third attempt of getting his attention he screamed his name, "RAFIKI!"

"What is it?" he said rudely. "I'm looking for the lion. If you shout like that it will draw him in to find us, so stop panicking as he is not around this part." Rafiki sounded pleased with himself that he had not put them in danger.

"Well, you're wrong," Roho stuttered. "I can see him, and he is getting closer! I think he thinks I'm his tea. GET ME OUT OF HERE!"

Just as he was about to pounce, Rafiki flapped his wings and said, "Home," and whoosh they were gone.

The lion pounced on nothing. He looked lost. Where had is food gone? It had never moved that fast before.

Roho was shaking when she got back to the enclosure. "I didn't realise we would be standing next to him! That was too close." She walked off sulking and stood by her mother in the giraffe house.

Rafiki sat on a branch and watched Roho. He hung his head low and thought that he may have just lost his best friend.

The next morning, Roho's nerves were on edge. Every time she heard a loud noise she turned around to see where it was coming from. In the distance she heard the lion roar and she rushed to her mother's side.

A child popped a crisp packet by blowing it up and squashing it in his hands. Roho rushed indoors when it went bang and refused to leave.

"What's up with you, Roho? You're very jumpy this morning," her mother said softly.

Roho nuzzled her neck against her mother's body. Her mother bent her neck to brush it on Roho's head.

Roho let out a contented sigh and closed her eyes and listened to her mother's breathing.

By the afternoon, Roho had calmed down and was outside with the other giraffes.

She had not seen Rafiki since last night.

Rafiki sat in his tree right at the top watching Roho all morning, too frightened to go down and say hello.

He could see how jumpy Roho was. Last night must have really scared her, more than he had realised.

He hoped he still had a best friend when he had the courage to go down and talk to her.

He listened to the children chatting below as they watched the giraffes.

"Why are giraffes' necks so long?" a child asked his friend.

"I don't know," she replied.

"Because they can't stand the smell of their feet," the child answered, bursting out laughing before running off to find their parents.

Rafiki laughed really hard and nearly fell off the branch. He had to start flying to keep his balance.

He landed on the giraffe's tree feeder where Roho was about to eat from.

"Oh, hello," Roho said to Rafiki.

"Hi, I have been worried you wouldn't talk to me again after last night." Rafiki smiled at Roho

"Well, I did think about it. I have been thinking a lot this morning. We need to work on your magic words before we go anywhere again."

"So you want to try again?" Rafiki was excited.

"Well yes, but not the lions!

Let's go for something that's not going to want to eat me for tea." Roho laughed but was still a bit nervous.

"Well," began Rafiki. "We could visit the monkeys, meerkats, hippos, then if you feel brave enough after those we could see the tigers, elephants—oh, there are so many to meet here in the zoo and that's just the big animals. There are lots of smaller ones to visit as well like the spiders."

Rafiki moved around excitedly thinking of their exciting new adventure.

About the Author

I live in West Sussex with my husband, daughter and our pets. I have been a childminder for many years and enjoy looking after children and reading them stories. When I'm not working I like to go for long walks with my dog along the beach or up on the Downs. The south coast is a beautiful place to live and grow up.

Acknowledgements

Thank you to Marina Greeves for you help in making the book come alive. My publishers for giving me the chance to show the world what I can do.